THE BUTTERFLY

AN ALPHA MALE CURVY WOMAN ROMANCE

SAVANNAH KOLE

CHAPTER 1

DARE

The definition of love lies different in everyone's dictionary of intellect. Some say it's something that saves you from the savagery of life, others describe it as hell on Earth; one that is inflamed by rejection and jealousy. Some people describe it as just a word that is the abstraction of something non-existent, a few old folks don't relate it to people. They relate the word to life itself, the joys of it. According to such people, there's a firm connection between love and faith in God.

But twenty-four year old Vanessa had no idea what love was. Precisely because she's been single for most of her life. Her friends often called her love life 'cursed'.

In high school she went to a private party, a mixer. There she met her first boyfriend, Jake. He broke up with her the exact day after stealing her first kiss. The reason revolved around the fact that she refused to give up her virginity so early; she was a little old school. Too 'boring' for the handsome guy who played basketball and showed off his buff body.

In college she dated a boy named, Joshua. Their relationship barely lasted two weeks because after visiting her house, he took an interest in her step-sister—who by the way—also found him sexy. They broke up right after she caught him cheating, too cliché, but that's the way it went. Well, Vanessa's sister found a fiancé as a result it and now they are about to get married by the end of the year. Vanessa was over it —she no longer hurt.

Not anymore.

After her bad experiences, she gave up on guys.

Especially the 'Js'.

She was a smart girl and so, she decided to devote her time to her studies and career. As a result, she graduated with the highest GPA in collage. Yeah, nerdy but at least her father finally noticed her presence. He was always busy showing his affection to his second wife and step children. Vanessa mostly felt left out in her family, she was eager to move out. Thankfully, she could do it all now.

"Congrats Nessa!"

Margaret, the only actual friend she

had in the group shouted while the bartender poured alcohol in their now empty cups. The remaining girls hooted along but deep down they were envious of Vanessa's coup.

"Thanks," Vanessa smiled while tasting the bitterness of vodka. This was her fourth shot.

Right after completing her internship, she applied at the *'BRD Group'*. The top company of US that also had branches in Europe and the middle east. They usually employed highly experienced professionals but the interviewer was impressed by Vanessa and decided to hire her.

"Well, living that flat life finally paid off," Bella commented.

She was this blonde, skinny girl who always walked in high heels. She grew up in the same neighborhood as Vanessa and so, they interacted often.

Her mother was the assistant editor of a well known gossip magazine.

"Yeah just like your chest," Vanessa mocked, while raising her little cup.

Bella's lower lip dropped low as she heard giggles from all around.

"What did you just say?" A thick nerve popped out of the side of her forehead that the other girls noticed, but Vanessa did not. She wasn't gonna go *there*.

"Can you deny it?" Vanessa continued to taunt. *Or maybe she did?*

Bella often talked down to her, but Vanessa was never the type to talk back. Margaret grinned while looking at Bella's face. Talks travel from girl to girl and so, Margret knew that Bella disliked Vanessa. The sole reason she decided to enter Vanessa's little party was to step on her happiness in some way, or to make her feel bad about her path.

"You used a dirty trick to crawl to

the top, didn't you?" Bella blurted while getting up, her hands were clenched into tight fists. Vanessa continued to take sips of her drink while smiling. "I will find out!" Bella held onto her Prada bag and walked away.

"She's just drunk," Alina, Vanessa's collage buddy commented.

Margaret already knew that Vanessa was not tolerant to alcohol. She barely took any, since this gathering was dedicated to her, she knew she needed to taste it. But now she couldn't stop drinking, she kept asking for more.

"Good water, please!" She kept the little glass in front of the bartender who didn't hesitate to pour in more. Margaret caught him passing weird smirks at her but she could not blame the guy. Vanessa usually looked plain because of her style which mostly consisted of oversized shirts and mom jeans. But once in a while, when she'd get ready, she would turn almost every head she'd walk by.

Her wavy brunette hair fell down to her waist, she wouldn't regularly get haircuts but the style suited her. The long black dress wrapped around her body like a second skin, added drama to her sultry curves. Vanessa was not skinny, nor was she your typical *fat*. She had a plump body that carried a pretty face.

"Let's play something." One of the girls proposed.

"Dare game?" Alina suggested immediately.

Vanessa turned around the moment she heard her friends. "Me first!" She volunteered to start the game. The girls started to think of a dare but Alina had already planned one for her. She tapped Vanessa's shoulder and pointed at the entrance door of the bar. It was somewhat dark inside and a lot of people rushed here and there, but the girls understood her direction.

"Your target is the first man who enters," Alina explained. "You need to bring his watch."

Vanessa frowned, "What if he's not wearing one?" She asked the obvious.

"I don't know, " Alina sputtered. "Ask for a little money or something."

Without actually replying, Vanessa got up. Before she could stand next to the door like a guard and wait for a random guy, someone entered while she was on her way. She couldn't quite see his face thanks to her blurry vision. She narrowed her eyes until he was completely visible to her. As she halted in front of the man, he also stopped walking.

Up close, he was probably the most handsome man Vanessa had seen in real life. He looked like the main character from those R-rated movies that become blockbusters. His suit, his dark hair, the shape of his beard, the spice of his reflective eyes, everything was *attractive*. Ignoring the two bodyguards that stood by his side, Vanessa stood hubristically.

"Please give me some money." Vanessa said the first thing that appeared in her mind. After giving it a slight thought, she quickly altered her statement. "I mean, your watch." She looked at his wrist. An expensive-looking piece encircled it.

"Why?"

"I don't know, it's totally not a dare." Her slight-bunny teeth enhanced her innocuous smile.

The man observed her by looking at her whole body, then stopped back at her face. An amused grin stretched above his jaw as he took his watch off.

"Cute," he complimented.

Vanessa rolled her eyes in the *I-know-I'm-cute* manner although ninety percent of the time she found herself *dingy*.

"Here," the man was about to hand her the watch but he stopped. "In exchange, tell me your name."

"Vanessa," she answered immediately. "Vanessa Baker."

He gave her the watch and then reached for his wallet. He was about to pull out some cash but Vanessa stopped him by holding his hand.

"No need, the watch is enough."

Vanessa rolled the watch around the tip of her finger without realizing that it cost more than her four year college tuition and bills combined.

"Shit, I think I'm going to throw up." Vanessa covered her mouth. While wearing the watch that rolled all the way to her elbow as it was too loose for her, she attempted to look for the bathroom despite having a cloudy mind.

The man observed her walk away,

something about the woman was odd, yet fascinating to him. Many women had approached him for his wealth but no one was as straight forward as *her*. On top of it, she didn't seem like she actually meant to attain an expensive watch.

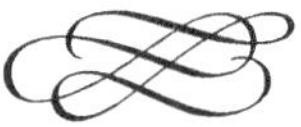

CHAPTER 2

DISASTROUS FIRST DAY

Vanessa closed the top button of her white shirt before wearing the jacket on top of it. She wore black pants that matched the jacket; some polyester suit she picked up at one of those discount stores. Vanessa's hair was tired into a clean ponytail, and she picked up her glasses and wore them before having a final look in the mirror.

She was about to grab her purse but her eyes stopped on the very watch she received from the stranger a few nights ago. A couple of days had passed, and she held onto it, the anxious feeling stirred her mind once again. After doing research the next day, she found out the *actual price* of the watch. She felt guilty, as if she had stolen an expensive good from someone. Margaret and the others assured her that the man gave it to her by his own free will, even Vanessa could remember the incident. But it still did not feel right.

Vanessa made up her mind to return it after finding the man who gave her the watch, she needed to return it. Because at the end of the day, she was a goodie. She was also a hard worker and would not want anything she didn't strive for. Her late mother taught her to trust merit and not easily achieved luxury.

Ignoring the bitter feeling in her pit, she placed the watch in her closet. It rested behind her bundle of cloths, and she closed the flaps. No one would usually be in her room, her step mom and sister barely interacted with her especially after the whole Joshua incident. Ironically, it was her sister, Aubrey that would get all cranky when Vanessa would hang out with them.

Leaving the clump of thoughts in her room, Vanessa stepped out and took a deep breathe. Today was the first day of her actual job, she was not going to let any negative ideas ruin it or disturb her while she worked and learn.

"Mr. Farrell, I've added another meeting to your schedule."

Jackson Farrell glimpsed over at his assistant before entering the building. The words somewhat infuriated him, Tyler Anderson could easily tell from his expressions.

"It's with your father, he's got something important to discuss," Tyler further elaborated. "Will you meet him tomorrow night?"

"Depends on my mood," Jackson bluntly replied.

As he walked by, many heads turned. Many of the bosses and presidents wanted to talk to him, for their own benefit and concerns, but Jackson hated useless talks. He only demanded work from these people, faultless work.

"Sir," Tyler wanted to say something more but Jackson raised his arm, he motioned for him to shut up.

Tyler really couldn't say anything more, listening to the CEO was *his* job. Jackson inherited his father's company a few years ago, ever since he took over, the empire only expanded and grew for the better. Even Jackson's father was shocked at the sudden gush of success that Jackson brought. Hard work wasn't all that it took, Jackson could thank his intellect. He was clever and competent, he was also dedicated. He dropped most of his social life for work.

Jackson would only meet up with his friends once a week, and he did not have a constant woman in his life. Not because they'd leave him—who would actually walk away from a hunky billionaire? He just couldn't stop at just one single woman. There were plenty of fish in the sea but he needed to try every single one of them so he could choose the finest, he stood by that idea. He didn't care about how many girls he left heartbroken, he would usually clear out his intentions and he wasn't looking for anyone long-term. But the other night, with the woman who asked for his watch—he went home *absorb by her* —blue eyes, dark long hair, curves everywhere, she was so his type!

"I'll meet you at the office in an

hour," Tyler proclaimed and waited for an 'ok', once he received it he turned around. He needed to attend a meeting on Jackson's behalf at the moment.

Jackson entered the elevator alone. The work hours had already begun and there weren't supposed to be many people rushing into the lift. Fate worked against his wishes and the elevator stopped right after he skipped a floor. As the doors slid open, he looked at the lady that strode inside.

After having a good look at her face, Jackson's heart sunk. *It was her!*

Vanessa kept staring at the digital map that was opened on her phone. Despite trying multiple times, she just couldn't figure out her department. Finally, she decided to get help from an actual person. She looked next to her and raised her chin to face the tall man. "Excuse me, would you know where the I-T Department is?"

Before he could answer, he watched her eyes go from *question mark* to *what-the-fuck* super fast. A sudden toll of anxiety took over her as she recognized him.

He was the very man she interacted with in the club?

"It's located on first floor," he said.

Vanessa felt dumb for entering the elevator, she was just on the first floor. *The man probably took her for a fool.*

"I know it gets confusing sometimes." He tried to relax her with his words. "New here?"

Vanessa accumulated a courageous smile and decided to continue the conversation. "Yes, I just joined today," she revealed. "Are you a regular worker?"

Jackson grinned, Vanessa could swear it was the most attractive smile she had ever witnessed.

"Yes."

"What's your name?" She only found it appropriate to ask for his name.

"Jackson Farrell."

Another Jay…

Vanessa stammered to start her next question. "Have we met?"

He smiled again, this time his teeth showed. The doors opened and he was about to step out.

"Later," he casually ignored her question, and walked away.

Throughout the early half of her first day, she could not concentrate well. All she could think of was that handsome gentleman that she was fortunate enough to interact with again. But she also found herself a little unfortunate because the very first meeting with him wasn't a pleasant one. Plus she needed to find a way to return his watch.

"Are you done?" Emily, a co-worker stopped by and asked.

Vanessa snapped out of her thoughts. "Ah, Yes!" She answered. For a second she admired Emily's light green eyes, they held a twinkle that blew out joy.

"It's break time," she informed while pointing at the wall clock. "Coffee?" She further invited.

"Sure!" Vanessa cleaned out her table by piling the paper on the side of her desk. While walking out and grabbing coffee, Vanessa thought, *would it be okay to ask her co-worker about Jackson?* "Can I ask you something?" She started.

"What's up?" Emily got off her phone, and faced Vanessa and was somewhat intimidated by her expressions. Vanessa looked nervous. "Is everything okay?"

"I met a guy this morning, I wanted to know where I could find him?"

Emily raised a brow. "And who might this guy be?"

"Would you really know about him?" Vanessa looked at the crowd of people in the cafeteria.

"Oh honey, I've been working here for *five* years. I know everyone," she reassured.

"His name is Jackson Farrell."

Emily stared at her blankly for a couple of seconds before laughing out loud, she even caught the attention of people sitting around them. The wild titter of the woman surely annoyed those who were looking for a couple of seconds of peace.

"No chance, he's out of your reach," Emily calmed a bit. "He has like, *crazy* standards for women."

Vanessa expected that, considering his looks. "No, I'm actually not interested in him." Vanessa exhaled a heavy breath, "it's just that I need to return something that belongs to him."

Her statement immediately caught Emily's attention, she leaned forward. "What thing?" She muttered with much curiosity.

Vanessa had just recently met Emily, but she seemed like a nice woman. She was professional in the office and festive out of it. She didn't find anything wrong in telling her a little bit about her problem.

"His watch."

"You have Jackson Farrell's watch?"

"Yes?"

"You're kidding, right?" Emily was stunned.

"I'm not." Vanessa tried to convince her. "Tell me, where can I find him?"

"Do you even know who he is?" Emily giggled a little out of shock that still surrounded her mind.

"An employee?"

"Would a regular employee give away his expensive watch?"

Emily's point was starting to hit Vanessa, she thought about it.

"Jackson Farrell is the CEO of the very company we stand in." Emily was clear with her words, no laughing or twirling the main case around.

Vanessa's jaw dropped low as she collected her memory. The fact that she demanded something from her *future boss*, while she was intoxicated with alcohol left her in great panic.

What type of impression did I leave on him?

It was her first day and she was already in deep trouble. At this point she started to expect an email with a termination letter in it. She quickly checked her phone and thankfully, she hadn't received it yet. She knew she needed to fix things—if she didn't stand up right now, she could endanger her future. Getting kicked out by a prominent company on her very first day would be career murder.

"Where is his office?"

CHAPTER 3

THEFT

Aubrey yawned while knocking on Vanessa's door. She was still sleepy but she needed to ask Vanessa for her floral dress before she decided to move out.

"Open up Vanessa!" She whined while still knocking.

"Vanessa's at work." Her mother walked by with new pot filled with sand. A little green shoot peeped in the middle, it was likely to grow in the next two weeks. Aubrey's mom loved growing plants. She was ready to place this new baby piece in their veranda.

As soon as Aubrey realized that Vanessa was away, she waited for their mother to walk away. Just as she did, Aubrey opened the door and entered her step-sister's room. She looked around, it was just as clean as ever. She switched her thoughts onto Vanessa's dress again, the yellow one. It was perfect for summer time and Aubrey needed it.

After going through the first rack of her closet, she moved to the next and finally found the bright color pop within the grays and blacks. She was about to grab it but something else caught her attention. It was something that radiated more than the sharp hue of yellow. It was a watch that looked brand new. It seemed like the ones Aubrey would see on T.V., the one's her fiancé would always want.

"Holy Molly, why does Vanessa have this?" She murmured to herself.

Aubrey held onto the piece and could immediately feel the originality. It was a men's watch, Aubrey's mind could not process the fact that her chunky sister held something like this. Aubrey remembered her lover, he would only die for a something like this. She knew he was very brand conscious. Without giving it much thought, Aubrey held tightly onto the watch and stood straight. She was not interested in the dress at all now, the valuable thing in her hand was enough to distract her mind. She didn't know exactly what she would do with it but she decided to keep it.

She closed the closet after perfecting the discipline of clothes in Vanessa's closet. She sneakily walked away and double checked the sound of any footsteps before stepping outside of the room. She walked away with much confidence, as if she had done nothing wrong.

After going through a few documents, Jackson faced the window. His office was located in the Penthouse. He could clearly see the traffic on the roads, next to which was a beautiful lake. The sky was illuminated with the sunlight, but the few fluffs of clouds claimed his mind. Being the CEO of such a big firm was not an easy job, he carried a lot of pressure on his shoulders. Although he had grown immune to the burden, he still wished he had someone important in his life. Someone he could lean on after a long tiring day, someone who would embrace his hand with the softness of hers.

But he just couldn't find that particular *her*.

Someone entered his office without knocking. Without turning around, Jackson already guessed who that person was.

"Sir?" Tyler called him out. "There's a new employee who wants to speak to you."

Jackson turned around upon hearing his words.

"We told her she can't, but she insists," He further explained.

Of course no one could meet Jackson Farrell without an appointment. In usual cases, Jackson would tell them to terminate the person but at this point he was actually waiting for her to approach him. Jackson was not the nicest to everyone but for some reason, he carried a soft spot for this particular woman and he could not understand why. "Let her in," he commanded.

Tyler was expecting a *no*, he was somewhat surprised to hear those words. It was at this very moment, Tyler realized something was off. Perhaps his boss knew this unknown girl waiting outside. Without speaking a word, Tyler walked out of the office and called Vanessa inside. He watched the timid looking woman enter the top man's office with no remorse, he could only imagine they needed to discuss something important.

Vanessa stopped a few steps away from Jackson's best, her eyes were fixed onto the floor. She kept taking small peeks at him, he was looking elsewhere.

"Tyler!" Jackson's call startled Vanessa instead of Tyler. His voice was deep and somewhat harsh. "You can leave." Vanessa watched as he ordered his assistant to step out of the office, it added to her nervousness. But she gulped down her skepticism and held her head high with much confidence. She was ready to face the man.

"Yes?" Jackson spoke.

Vanessa cleared her throat before speaking, as if she was about to demonstrate a presentation to her boss, which was definitely the case.

"We met on Friday night, right?" She brought up the topic.

Jackson grinned. "Yes, I remember."

Vanessa snickered a little until she recalled who she stood in front of, she could not be this carefree around the CEO.

"I'm sorry, I wasn't in my right mind at that time," she reasoned.

Jackson nodded, the slight dimple on his right cheek was still visible. "How was your first day?" He slid away from the topic almost as he was avoiding the conflict.

Vanessa thought it odd he would ask, "My first day?"

Jackson grinned then looked down at his paperwork. "Yes, how was your first day?" He repeated.

"It was nice," she said, with a big smile but her tone eventually faded low. "Your company is good."

"Good?" He repeated the last word. "I see."

"Mr. Farrell, there's something I'd like to discuss." Vanessa fiddled with her fingers behind her back. "Do you have the time?" She asked out of concern.

"Time?" Jackson moved towards his seat and settled down. "I have much time, for you."

Vanessa felt a little blush on her cheek upon hearing the charming guy's remark, but she realized it was something normal for him.

"I was dumb and acted foolish," she started by admitting her faults. "The watch I asked for is great, but I can't keep it."

"Why not?" He questioned, he sounded a little concerned.

"Well, first off—it's male's watch." She naturally spoke. "I mean I can't possibly *wear* it."

"Oh, is that it?"

"Also, I can't keep something I didn't work to get." She finished.

Jackson remained quiet for a few seconds, he was somewhat impressed by the girl's morals. She was the type who could deny a castle of gold if she couldn't buy it with her own money. She was a different type of beautiful, one that attracts the soul. "Very well," Jackson nodded.

Vanessa took it as a *yes*. "Them I'll return it to you tomorrow."

"Don't bring it in the office."

Vanessa raised the inner corners of

her eyebrows as she failed to understand why.

"If employees hear about it, they'll get the wrong idea."

"Oh," she nodded as she understood.

"We'll meet somewhere outside, okay?" He sounded like he'd already made the decision.

Vanessa did not have a problem with it. "Sure."

Upon hearing her response, Jackson took out his phone and handed it to her. "Your number," he demanded.

By this time, he stood close to her, and Vanessa stared into his eyes for a good couple of seconds before finally grabbing the phone. While doing so, her finger touched his hand, and at that moment she noticed a smirk on his lips.

A peculiar feeling hit her, but she ignored it for now. All she needed to do was return the watch, then she could start being a normal employee at the company. She'd probably never interact with the CEO again.

Somehow the thoughts of not talking to him after everything was settled made her meloncholy.

CHAPTER 4

"Who do you think is responsible for this?"

A middle-aged woman who wore a baggy brown shirt spoke in a surprisingly low tone, considering how pissed off she was at the moment. Her husband sat opposite to her, in his grasp was an almost empty bottle of alcohol. His hair were messy and he'd been wearing the same shirt for the past four days.

"Answer me!" She shouted with

much remorse in her voice. As if she had been gulping down the hate for a long while. The screech in her voice reflected her feelings well as she gaped at her husband. In response the man threw the glass bottle at her, she dodged it fortunately.

"Get me another one," he ordered.

His mindset was unstable at the moment, he could only think about himself. His wife was specifically mad at that, but she was more concerned about the blunder he recently committed.

"Is everything okay?"

The blonde boy who went by the name of Joshua stepped downstairs while taking off his headset. He knew damn well another circus was about to go around in their little apartment, he also knew there was not much he could do.

"This old man gambled again!" His woman complained to her son.

Joshua rubbed the temples of his head. "How much did he take this time?"

"All of our savings!"

Joshua was left perplexed, he went through trouble processing the information. Their savings consisted of all the money his mother and he collected in order to start a small business. That vision was the only source of hope for the boy.

Before he could throw his clenched fists at his aged father for ruining his goal, the bell started to ring. Although he only wanted to deal with his family at the moment, he'd already promised Aubrey that he would spend time with her. He did not predict a good time anymore.

Aubrey entered and could feel the tension in the air. Joshua's mother lit her cigarette while staring at the floor while his father laid on the sofa like a junkie. Joshua didn't appear in a good mood either. Aubrey's greeting went ignored before the couple walked upstairs and entered Joshua's room.

"Things aren't going good here."

"What happened?" She raised a brow while helping him settle down.

"All the money is gone," Joshua started. "I won't be able to open the café anymore."

Aubrey covered her mouth, she was also shocked. She could tell only his father could be responsible for this.

"If I'm not financially stable, I don't think we can get married." He quickly turned the topic towards *her*. He knew only she could get him out of the mess. He considered her clever, he believed she could find a way out of every trouble.

"This must be fate," Aubrey's sincere smile left Joshua concerned.

She leaned over to wipe away the few drops of sweat that had gathered on his forehead and held his hand. "Babe, I have a way out of this."

CHAPTER 5

DATE

"He asked you to meet him outside?" Margret could not believe her ears. Vanessa needed to repeat her words again.

"Yes, I just received the address." She looked at the screen of her phone, Margret snatched the device away.

"No way!" She sounded way more excited then Vanessa, who was actually going to meet him.

Vanessa sent confirmation message to Jackson, which he immediately saw.

As if he was waiting for her reply. "'It's nothing too big," Vanessa scoffed.

"Where's the location? It's a restaurant isn't it?"

"How did you know that?" Vanessa asked, a little confused.

"He's literally taking you on a date," Margret implied. "Why would such a busy person make time out of his schedule to meet you?"

"There's a valid reason."

"Don't make me laugh, he doesn't care about the watch."

Vanessa looked in the mirror while running her hands through her hair, she was getting nervous. Speaking to Margret was making it worse. Deep down she knew there was something going on inside Jackson's mind, but she did not want to believe in anything. She wanted to consider her thoughts and hope just a bundle of misunderstandings and delusions.

"I don't have a chance with him." She whispered while looking at herself. She did not consider herself all that pretty, her thighs were obese and she was nowhere near skinny. There were thousands of women out there that were prettier and more suitable for Jackson Farrell. As a drop of insecurity fell on her heart, she took a deep breath.

"What?" Margret could hear her murmurs.

"Nothing!" She smiled cheerfully while walking towards her closet. "I don't want to be late." She opened the doors and searched for the piece of metal, but her hand couldn't reach out to the watch. A fright trembled her heart as she continued to throw out clothes in her search.

Her quick movements worried Margret and she walked over to her.

"I can't find it!" Vanessa cried out.

Vanessa had refused to let him pick her up because her house was so far away from his. She recommended it would be the best if they both meet up at the decided place. After waiting for about five minutes, Jackson finally spotted Vanessa. He could not take his eyes off her. When he first met her, he couldn't have a good look at her because of the flashy club lights. But at this moment, she approached him in a beautiful green dress that displayed her body perfectly. It wasn't too revealing but the neckline was low, Jackson could see other men looking at the woman who was meant to meet him. It boiled his blood to see someone else smirk while looking at her but her subtle beauty claimed his heart, once more. Her hair bounced with every swing of her hips, they looked like a brown stream of silk that reached her waist.

"Hi," she spoke.

Jackson felt as if her confidence was somehow lowered. He stared into her ocean blue eyes and found a tint of green in them.

"Hey Vanessa, take a seat." Jackson looked at the empty chair in front of him, she was quick to settle down on it.

"How are you, Sir?" Vanessa began talking.

"Good," he answered. "And don't call me *Sir*, you can call me Jackson."

"Okay," she giggled. "Jackson." She called his name in a fancy accent but ended up realizing she was being too friendly with a man who is actually the boss of her boss's boss.

"For such a little thing, you arranged a whole dinner. Thank you." Vanessa made her appreciation visible before she could break down the news for him: she did not bring the very thing they met for.

"This is my favorite restaurant, I wanted to dine here tonight. Having a young intellectual only adds to the enjoyment."

Before she could respond to his praise, the waiter started to arrange the food and while doing so, he chatted with Jackson.

"I see you brought a woman this time," he remarked, while looking at Vanessa.

Vanessa smiled awkwardly. She didn't know what to say but the same thoughts kept rotating around her intellect. He doesn't usually bring women here. *Why me?*

Once the man left, they talked while finishing dinner. Jackson discussed a number of topics with Vanessa, including world affairs, business and politics.

"You really are smart, no wonder you were selected despite not having much experience." Jackson sipped onto champagne after saying so, his eyes did not leave her sight even for once. They were fixed on her for the past thirty minutes, Vanessa would occasionally look away when it'd become too much for her to handle. The man was gorgeous, she faced problems controlling her the speed of her elevated heartbeat.

"Thanks," Vanessa responded, displaying her perfect set of white teeth.

"Beauty with brains," he added.

Why did he say such things? Vanessa had never received this much attention from a man before! Vanessa felt her cheeks warm up and it was not because of the wine. Her head started to feel a little heavy as her heart started to beat faster. Jackson was not at a great distance, in fact the table was not that long. Leaning forward, he tucked a strand of her hair behind her ear. He could feel the heat of her skin as his cold fingers brushed past her cheeks and touched her ear.

"Jackson?" Her muscles tensed up as she stared back at him with wide eyes.

"Let's hang out more often."

"Why?"

"So, I can get to know you better."

"And then?"

"If things work out, I will make you my wife."

What the hell?!

That was it—a sense of disquietude within her shot up. She could not believe her ears. With a smile on his face, he really said those words. Jackson stood up with his hands in his pocket, the blue suit stretched out around his shoulders; he was an aesthetic sort of charismatic. His phone started to buzz and he looked at it before glancing at Vanessa.

"Should I drop you home?"

Vanessa took a few seconds to process his question. "No, I'm good."

She was okay with taking an Uber. Actually, that would be better considering the talk they just had.

"Well, take care."

Vanessa nodded before he walked away. Right after he left the room, Vanessa put her head down on the table while covering it with her hands. "What the fuck—"

In the midst of this new incident, the whole watch thing was not even brought up. Vanessa realized the actual thing he wanted to talk to her about was *this. His wife? Was he kidding? What sort of sick prank was this anyhow?*

• • •

At a distance of few tables, a woman sat with crossed legs. A smile painted on her face—it wasn't a happy one, nor was it a sad. It was the sign of retribution.

"Now I understand how you got the job," Bella spoke to herself while looking at Vanessa.

CHAPTER 6

FINALLY FOUND

"I've put it online, let's wait." Aubrey looked at the screen of her laptop while sitting on Joshua's bed. Joshua held the watch in his hands.

"We're going to sell it to the highest bidder," Joshua said, while walking in circles. "It looks brand new, after all." He reasoned.

"Of course!" Aubrey agreed.

Her phone started to ring, she looked at the name before putting it on silent and throwing it away.

"Who is it?" Joshua asked in concern.

"Your ex-girlfriend," Aubrey rolled her eyes while saying so. Joshua immediately understood what she meant but he looked at her screen just to confirm.

"Vanessa, I see."

"Who else?"

"She keeps calling me, obviously she noticed the absence of that watch." Aubrey rubbed the temples of her head, "I haven't even gone home, I know she's suspecting me."

"Not that her suspicion is wrong," Joshua grinned, teasing her.

"I'm doing this for you," Aubrey said, crossed her arms.

"Chill babe, I was kidding."

Aubrey rolled her eyes, there were times Joshua appeared as the most annoying person on Earth to her. But at the end of the day, she loved him unconditionally.

"Where did she get something like this?" Joshua expressed his curiosity.

"Who knows? She does work with rich people now." The girl implied, she held on the pillow on her left and threw it at Joshua with full force. Almost as if she wanted to murder the man with the softest thing in the room.

"You went to the same college as her!"

"So?"

"Look at the difference in your careers." Aubrey grunted but Joshua found it cute.

"Except I don't have one."

Vanessa stood in the restroom of her office with a huge frown stretched across her forehead. She looked at her phone, Aubrey was not picking it up. It was obvious she took it by now, Vanessa knew Aubrey would only contact her after selling the watch and then act like she did not do it. It infuriated her. "Shit."

Vanessa splashed some water on her face. Before she could realize it, Emily walked in out of nowhere. She raised her chin to look at Vanessa who was a bit taller than her.

"Is everything okay?"

Vanessa shook her head with a fake smile. "Yes, I just felt a little tired."

"Do you think I believe that?"

"What?"

"I can tell something is bothering you."

Vanessa looked down and let out a bothered sigh.

Jackson sighed while attending the phone call, it was from the one person he did not want to talk to. It was not because he hated this man, but the related bilateral issues they faced as a family.

"Hello father."

"Why didn't you meet me last night?" Jackson's father cut the long talk and got to the point.

"I was busy."

"With that employee of yours?"

Jackson got up from his chair as he heard those words. His father was not supposed to know about *that*.

"I know you wanted to talk about my marriage with one of your old friends." Jackson diverted the direction of the talk. "I really wasn't up for that."

"My old friends?" His father phrased before storming into a loud laughter. He took a few breaths before calming himself down. "Do you know how much we could benefit from their companies?"

"I don't let anyone decide for me, even if its you." Jackson was nowhere near giving up to his father's greed despite having a pool of money.

"Erase your relations with the working girl," his father demanded, referring to Vanessa. "If this issue gets out, it'll be big trouble."

The call got cut from the other side before Jackson could speak a few words. Tyler entered the office that instant with a few files that he decorated on his own table that stood by the corner of the office.

"Your father released his anger on me last night when you skipped the meeting with him." Those were the first words of communication that Tyler used today.

Jackson settled back on his chair.

"Going after that girl won't be worth

it, she's an employee." Tyler was probably the only person Jackson trusted with his life in this building. The only reason why he was taking Mr. Farrell's side in this was to save Jackson from unwanted trouble. Truthfully, it would create a lot of problems if people found out he was hanging around with a lowly co-worker.

"So, you're against relationships between a boss and worker?" Jackson asked, with a little grin.

Tyler stopped managing the papers and glanced at Jackson.

"What did Emily say?" Jackson asked, curious.

Tyler sighed before getting back at work. "We made up. She asked me to take her to a movie next time."

"I'm not talking about your silly fights." Jackson turned his chair towards his assistant's direction. "What did she say about Vanessa?"

"Right." Tyler hid his embarrassment by busying himself even more in his work while words continued to slip his mouth. "She's getting a little closer to her. In fact, Vanessa has talked about you."

"What did Vanessa say?" Jackson interested.

"Nothing romantic—that's for sure."

"Elaborate."

"Looks like Vanessa is really concerned about returning your watch."

Jackson recalled the whole matter, he was so focused on thinking about his time with her he actually forgot about that.

"She wants to return it but she can't." Tyler awoke a curiosity within his Boss. "Looks like her sibling stole it."

Jackson understood his statement and started to snicker. "Poor people really fight over that shit, how pitiful."

Tyler tilted his head.

"Of course, Vanessa is different. She carries herself with grace."

"In all honesty I don't know what you see in her, she appears to be pretty mediocre to me," Tyler casually stated. He was not actually trying to insult Vanessa, rather trying to find out Jackson's main source of interest. He wanted to know why his cold Boss was suddenly doing all the things he's never done before.

Jackson looked closely at the screen of his computer, a live CCTV footage was playing. Vanessa entered the department and got into her seat. She was typing with much concentration, just like how Jackson was looking at her.

"Vanessa is a different type of gorgeous," Jackson complimented.

At that moment, Tyler realized something; his Boss was not going to give up on this woman until he got her. And if he couldn't get her in the usual way, he would be willing to go to all kinds of lengths. The thought was a little scary but he brushed it off. Tyler hoped the woman would devote herself completely, because the other way around would not be pretty. Of course, he was going to use his secret girlfriend in order to achieve that.

CHAPTER 7

The working hours were almost over and Vanessa was trying her level best to finish everything before the official leave time. She cracked her knuckles and stretched her neck before jumping her fingers back onto the keyboard. Her typing was pretty fast, she liked working, she liked the rapid clicking sound it created as a result. She wanted to impose a good impression on her seniors for her first project.

Emily was one of her seniors, she was helping her a lot in the office.

Vanessa often wondered why Emily was so friendly and supportive to her. In a world filled with people who only worked for themselves and their advantages, Vanessa was understanding of this.

"Done?"

The woman that encompassed Vanessa's mind appeared before her very eyes with her usual smile.

"Yep," Vanessa answered while saving her file.

Emily leaned against her table while tapping her long nails on the metal. Vanessa looked at her co-worker who was slowly turning into her friend, and decided to spill her thoughts.

"Why are you being so nice to me?"

"'Cause you look like a friendly girl," Emily smiled, she looked prepared for the question. "When I first joined this place, I was about your age. As someone completely new, I really needed someone to support me." Emily was looking elsewhere while talking because in reality, it was a lie. "So, when I saw you, I knew you held similar thoughts."

Vanessa held a blank expression until she realized her point. She was not the type to witness others express their feelings for her and so, she felt a little embarrassed. "Damn you talk like you're an old woman," Vanessa joked, to which she received a slow hit on her shoulder.

"Move." Emily pushed Vanessa's chair away along with her while leaning towards the computer. Vanessa watched, as her new friend opened some website and continued to search for something. She really wondered what could be so important to look for at this moment.

"I found it," Emily smiled, while moving away. "I think so."

The screen was clear to Vanessa now

and she moved closer to have a good look. It was some sort of online shop. The product on sale was the same model of watch she had lost.

"Wait, is this the same one?" Vanessa wondered as a little doubt remained in her heart.

"The seller's name is Joshua Clarkson. He lives around here." Emily pointed at the information. "Does this ring a bell?"

"Joshua?" Vanessa asked in disbelief. "I can't believe they would stoop this low."

"Is he related to you?"

"He's my step-sister's fiancé," Vanessa answered.

"Oh, I see," Emily understood. "Partners in crime, are they?"

"I'll deal with it, thank you for helping." Vanessa stood up and pulled Emily into a tight hug.

Emily tapped her back, she felt a

little weird. She did not have many female friends. Actually, after her friendship broke off with her old best friend, she did not make *any* female friends. She merely approached Vanessa because Tyler asked her to, but now, she was not regretting it.

CHAPTER 8

*J*oshua kept checking his phone after regular intervals of time – about every fifteen minutes. A lot of buyers contacted him but no one proposed the price he was seeking. He needed a good amount of money in order to start his business.

His mother walked out of her room. Despite being stuck in a financial crisis, her hair was still curled into rollers. She liked taking care of herself. "Where is your old man?"

"I don't know, probably gambling again."

"What does he have left?" She scoffed while settling on the couch in front of the T.V.

"Who knows?"

One thing Joshua admired about his father, and gamblers in general was the hope in their spirit. They always held onto it, thinking a sudden luck would change their life. As for people like Joshua, neither did they have faith in luck nor hope. They simply depended on others.

The doorbell started to ring. Joshua guessed it was either his father or Aubrey since she had left to grab some groceries. To his surprise, it was not her, but someone he did not expect. He just stared at Vanessa, and felt a lump suddenly stuck in his throat. He could not utter a single word. It was that feeling you get when you're caught red handed.

"Where is Aubrey?" She asked.

Joshua gulped before finally talking. "I don't know, she's not here." Vanessa was not buying it and it was visible in her eyes. "You can check the house if you don't believe me!" Joshua stepped away while opening the door wide.

"Perfect," Vanessa said, as Joshua quickly realized that she could find the watch in his room. He blocked the way right after she had taken one step. "Why do you want to see her?"

"You two have something that belongs to me." She was bold with her words and the tone that carried them.

"What might that be?" He acted clueless.

Vanessa slid her phone open and opened a screenshot. She held the phone an inch away from his eyes and he had to move back in order to have a good look. It was the selling page of the goods. Vanessa could tell Joshua was getting nervous.

"So, what?" He stuttered.

"This was stolen from my closet."

Joshua looked away. Vanessa studied next to him for many years, she knew his personality. He was not that confident, he always needed strong people to stand next to him in order to hold him up. If Aubrey were here, she would have handled the situation like a pro.

"Vanessa," he finally looked into her eyes. "Do you have any proof?"

"What?"

"Do you have any proof that we stole it?" His voice cracked a little as he asked. But he was slowly starting to make valid points in the debate. "You don't, right?"

Vanessa pitied him. She could tell he desperately need the money for something and was ready to make up any old reason to justify his actions. "You've learned a few dirty tricks from her," Vanessa voiced, while clenching her teeth. She would not force them to hand something over if it was not related to her pride. She made a promise, she needed to return that watch.

"If you don't have proof, then go away."

"Joshua—give it to me."

"I will tell the police you're trying to take something that belongs to us. Your father would not like hearing about that."

"You are a horrible person," she reacted, feeling helpless.

"I need the money," Joshua finally admitted.

Before their exchange of words could continue, a lavish car stopped outside his house. Vanessa watched from the large living room window as a man in a suit approached the front door. He was somewhat charming; his blonde hair was combed back and a few strands fell on his forehead. Vanessa could swear she'd seen him somewhere.

He knocked on the door and Joshua quickly answered it.

"Hi, I'm Tyler Anderson," he said, introducing himself, shaking hands with Joshua. "I came to buy the watch."

"How much are you bidding?" Joshua asked, quickly.

"How much do you prefer?"

"Fifty-thousand dollars."

"Done," Tyler pulled out his checkbook while saying so.

"Right now?" Joshua's question went unanswered as Tyler continued to sign the check. "Please come inside." Joshua invited him.

"No, bring it here."

Joshua nodded, as he tried to pick

up his dropped jaw. Everything was happening lightning-fast as he looked at Vanessa. "Please ignore my sister-in-law, she's sick in the head."

"The watch?" Tyler asked with a straight face.

Joshua nodded before running through the living room and towards his room upstairs.

"Mr. Anderson, you can't buy it. It belongs to someone else," Vanessa spoke up, as she watched him ignoring her.

The moment Joshua returned, he demanded the check. Upon receiving it, he handed the watch to Tyler who then gave it *to* Vanessa.

"Excuse me?" Joshua asked, bewildered.

Tyler smiled. "The money was given to you as a Grant through a popular program our company runs."

"Huh?"

"We're helping the needy." A smile coated Tyler's thin lips with a hint of mockery. "Someone reported that you were troubled. This watch is now with its rightful owner."

Tyler tapped Joshua's shoulder before walking towards his car. "Vanessa, do you need a ride somewhere?"

Vanessa could tell the unknown man just helped her get the watch back but she failed to understand why.

"I see you're having fun with rich people," Joshua mocked, as he understood the situation. "Watch out, they might just bite you."

Vanessa watched as he closed the door halfway, his eyes did not leave her. "Anyone's better than a *cheater*."

Vanessa did not hold grudges but she kept a clear memory. In no way could she forget all that happened years ago.

Back then, she was not totally in love with Joshua but she still held strong feelings for him. The worst part was the feeling of not being enough for someone. She changed her ways, her attitude, she even went to the gym. She changed her friends for him, but he was still quick to leave her for someone else. It hurt knowing someone replaced her flaws with love for another. She was over him now, she forgave, but she did not forget.

Tyler honked and the loud noise immediately made Vanessa turn around. She opened the door and settled onto the passenger's seat.

"So, who are you?" She asked, as he began driving.

"I believe you know my name now, I'm Mr. Farrell's assistant, Tyler Anderson?"

He introduced his position, Vanessa had trouble connecting the dots.

"Don't worry about the money, it was taken from granting funds."

As if he could read her mind, he answered one of her questions. Before she could flood him with more questions, Vanessa looked down at the watch. She touched the metal, knowing this could be the last time she held it.

"Can you take me to see Mr. Farrell?"

"Sure, I believe you have something you need to return," Tyler said, while speeding up the car.

CHAPTER 9

THE TRUTH

Jackson walked into his living room just to find the gem he was searching for; the breeze to his heart sitting there. He received a message from Tyler that he was dropping Vanessa over but Jackson was still amazed by her presence.

She made his soul smile, he made her heart beat.

Minutes before, Vanessa was in awe of his fine furnishings, ornate rugs and expensive oil paintings. "Hello, Mr. Farrell," Vanessa said, sweetly.

She used his last name on purpose, it was a sign of distance. She did not refer to him as *Jackson*, she was not here to be flirty at all. "Hello, Miss Baker," he tested her.

He sat down on the sofa next to her, she held a blank expression opposite to her jumping heartbeat. "I came to return this," Vanessa explained, laying the watch on the table in front of them.

Jackson looked at it for merely a second. "Thank you."

"How did you know about the sale?" She questioned, in all seriousness.

"What?"

"You know exactly what I'm talking about."

Jackson noticed the determination in her eyes, she wanted answers.

"Did you send someone to tail me?" She crossed her arms. "Or was it Emily?"

Jackson was galvanized by her quick-witted mind, he was not expecting her to figure it out with such speed.

"Wow." His lips curved.

"Is it easy for you to play with other's lives?" She stood up. A fiery anger boggled up in her mind. She was hurt by the fact that Emily only got close to her so she could pass information onto the man who was timely obsessing over her. Knowing he could get anyone to enter her life just because of his power and money made her bite onto her lip.

"Vanessa," he cajoled, feeling bad.

"I found you nice," she admitted, on the verge of emotion. "I don't anymore." Vanessa felt as if she were losing something, her heart was breaking and she couldn't stop the pain.

As Jackson watched her walk away, every nerve in his body told him to stop her. She was like a beautiful butterfly to him, one he wanted to cage for himself if she didn't choose him on her own free will. The thought of losing her to another man made his blood run cold, he would murder the person if necessary. No, that wouldn't do.

Jackson beat her to the door as she reached for the knob. Twirling her body around, he made her face him.

Anger to heat.

Passion to sexual desire.

He bore into her eyes—and he could instantly see it. Fire enough to burn. Daring to taste her lips, he bent down to her pucker and sucked her in.

Uncontrolled sensuality never tasted so sweet.

Vanessa opened her eyes as his lips left hers. "Why did you do that?"

Watching her chest heaving up and down, he whispered, "I had to stop you somehow."

Vanessa grinned, she liked how he

just took control—and took her—she wanted more. "I have to go."

Jackson grabbed her hand, "Stay the night with me? You can leave in the morning?"

Vanessa tilted her head, "Why?"

Jackson brushed his lips across hers once more, only this time, lightly and with less force. Whispering into her face, he said softly, "Because whether you realize it or not, you're mine Vanessa Baker."

Vanessa's resolve melted on the spot. She didn't want to fight it anymore and wrapped her arms around his handsome shoulders. Kissing him deeply, she pushed passed his tongue and with hers, danced a fiery tango.

Breaking apart from her kiss, he grabbed her other hand and led them to his bedroom. Pushing her down on the bed, he heard her giggle deep in her throat. He wanted her naked, now.

She was wearing one of those wrap-around dresses, the ones that tied in the front and with one quick yank, the whole dress sprung open wide. She was wearing a red bra and lace panties and that turned him on even more.

Vanessa watched Jackson, as he discarded his T-shirt up over his head and pulled down his jeans to expose his boxers and an erection she couldn't wait to feel.

Vanessa watched him as he knelt on the bed and darted towards her breasts. He seemed enthralled with exposing her skin and watched with amazement as he slid down her bra straps to reveal two large perky mounds. Lowering his head into her left breast, he cupped her skin and suckled and licked until she was wet and hot and ready for him.

Opening up her legs with his knees, she felt him enter—rock hard, large, thick—and pumping her in all the right places. She wrapped her legs around his waist and accepted his weight into her crux as he continued to pay homage to her nipples and felt the most delicious sensation bloom and spread straight down to her toes.

Waiting to feel her climax end, Jackson picked up both her thighs and began to pump her even harder. Pumping and fucking her until he heard her yelp again!

God, he couldn't get enough of her! Her tight pussy, her wide thighs, her two large breasts, her protruding nipples—she was like a sexual narcotic!

Thrusting one last time, he spilled his seed inside of her—totally forgetting about his condom. *Fuck the condom,* he wanted this woman—now! His wife, *his* —would she accept his proposal again?

CHAPTER 10

WHAT THIS LOVE?

A few days had passed.

Emily stopped by her co-worker who was dealing with some online work. The man halted right the moment he noticed her hour glass figure. Emily did not like chit-chatting usually, she wore a solemn look.

"Mr. Eric, are there any problems?" She questioned while fixing her hair.

"None at all, I've looked online and all of them are posting in our favor." He answered while making his voice sound deeper.

"Stay on track you know today is important, right?"

"Of course."

Emily was referring to the latest project launched by their company, it was a big step towards expanding the empire. A new building was set up in California as a part of their tourism project. It was a grand hotel that took a whole year to build, it was located at an ideal holiday location. If something inappropriate was to spread online regarding the company, the project could have a bad start and a potential loss.

"Keep working hard," she instructed, giving him the smile he was thirsty for.

Quite a few men in the office took an interest in Emily around the building. They always found her introverted behavior towards them a little weird, some swore she was already dating someone, possibly even gay.

The clicking sound of Emily's heels stopped the moment she noticed Vanessa, who glimpsed at her for a second before moving towards her space.

Emily was about to swallow her pride once more and take steps towards her but then the realization hit her again: Vanessa was not going to listen. Over the past couple of days Emily tried multiple times to reach out to Vanessa but she refused to talk about anything other than work.

Vanessa was about to hop onto her seat when a foreign worker entered their space, the woman walked towards Vanessa with a smile.

"Mr. Farrell wants to see you," she conveyed.

Her co-workers sitting next to her

gasped in shock. The CEO was personally calling a worker?

"Tell him, I'll be there in a sec," Vanessa said, typing at her computer again. She was ready to murder the keyboard with all the tension rising up inside of her. But she hid it with a calm expression.

"What do you want?" She asked, right after entering his office.

"That's not how you talk to your boss," he cajoled, leaning back in his desk chair.

"Mr. Farrell, how can I help you?" She faked a smile.

"By walking closer."

Every passing second felt like a rope tightening around her abdomen. The more she tried to resist him, the worse it twisted. Without spitting a single word, Vanessa walked closer to him. The only way to stop this feeling of discomfort was by talking to him. She still was not over everything, she still needed time. After the crazy sex they had, Jackson asked her to marry him —*again*. Feeling so over-whelmed, Vanessa gathered up her belongings and ran away. It was only today that she's seen him. She ignored his calls and he had been tied up with meeting after meeting.

But good lord, the scent of his strong cologne caused a tsunami between her legs.

Vanessa had only been a few short feet away. Jackson leaned over and grabbed at her clothes and drew her near. Sitting in his chair still, he bore up into her blue eyes. "We're not done, you and I."

Vanessa bit down on her lower lip, she wanted to suck on his tongue again. "You've given me a lot to think about."

She was lighting the inferno again and he stood up, lifted her body and pushed her onto his table, all the while suffocating her lips with his. Her heavy breathes were echoing through out the room. He moved from her lips to her neck and nibbled on the chunks of her skin, a moan erupted from her mouth as she held tightly onto his white shirt. He let go of her and took his suit jacket off, then loosened his tie.

His hand unbuttoned her shirt and fondled her breast.

Vanessa could not think straight at the moment, she felt herself indulging into something out of the universe, an endless bliss. Once her belt loosened up, her pants followed and Jackson's fingers tickled her inner thighs, smirking while looking at her expressions.

"Do you want it?" His low, guttural whisper gave her goosebumps.

She nodded, "Yes."

"Blame me later," he let go, touching her bud as his fingers drenched in her honey. Vanessa's lips parted as she curved into his thrust. He began to unzip his own pants.

Just then someone barged in.

"Mr. Farrell?"

The muscles around Jackson's jaw tensed up as he turned around to face Tyler, who quickly understood the situation and walked out.

Vanessa wiggled away from his fingers, and pulled her pants back up. "I think it was something important."

"How do you know?"

"He wouldn't have barged in, he would have knocked."

"Tyler *never* knocks," Jackson said, buttoning Vanessa's blouse back up.

Vanessa looks deep into his eyes, "Work comes first, right?"

"You're my top priority right now," he said, grabbing her hand to allow her to feel the rise in his crotch.

She clicked her tongue, "I'll want that later, thank you very much."

"You'll get this and plenty more," Jackson leered down at her.

Vanessa smiled and gave him a peck on the lips, "Call him back in."

"You're sure?"

"More than sure."

Jackson went to his telephone intercom and buzzed his assistant back into his office.

Leaning up against Jackson's desk, Vanessa watched Tyler walk in and clear his throat.

"So, what was the emergency?" Jackson asked, his arms crossed across his chest.

Tyler, kept glancing at Vanessa.

She felt a little embarrassed, as he had seen them earlier, possibly skin.

"Mr. Farrell, someone released an article about you and her," Tyler quickly expressed. "*Starlife,* the magazine—they've got photos of you two."

The name quickly clicked in Vanessa's mind. "Starlife? That's where Bella's mom works."

"Who is Bella?" Jackson asked, baffled.

Vanessa rolled her eyes, "Oh, she's some girl who's always had it out for me."

"So, you know them?" Jackson's attention shifted towards Vanessa.

"Yes."

{{{BUZZZZ}}}

Jackson's and Tyler's office telephones started to ring, along with their personal cell phones. Even Vanessa's started to buzz.

It was happening.

Jackson turned his attention towards Vanessa again. Setting down his phone, he grabbed at her hands. "This nonsense isn't going away anytime soon."

Vanessa locked eyes with his. "I see that now."

"So, what is it?"

Tyler is confused. "What is *what*? You guys are speaking in riddles! We have a small crisis here!"

Vanessa smiled and gave Jackson a small peck on the lips. "She's going to marry him."

THE END

ACKNOWLEDGMENTS

Thank You for reading, "The Butterfly"
- An Alpha Male Curvy Woman
Romance

If you liked this book, please leave a
positive book review

YOU MIGHT ALSO LIKE

MYSTIQUE

When Becca Jones has a flat tire, she receives help from none other than her obnoxious white neighbor. He's charming, he's handsome, but Becca doesn't take the bait.

Aiden Holmsted is a millionaire tech wizard who has a crush on the dark beauty. But she's standoffish, mysterious and doesn't accept his help right away.

Unforeseen coincidences continually push them together until sparks fly and the mystery, clears.

Find humor and love with Becca and
Aiden
in this
Black Woman White Man Romance!

TAUNT ME

Jason Ryan just resumed work as the CEO of his late father's company after his old man got killed by a drunk black man. Under strict instruction from his father's will to work with the carefully selected employees on the team or stand being replaced, Jason feels he got the bad end of the deal especially when he has to deal with his infuriating black secretary.

Devoted secretary, Kyra Aston is nothing short of a perfectionist. Unfortunately, due to the death of her former boss, her path collides with that of his son who is a hard worker but hates black people. Working with him is a nightmare and she wants so much to leave.

Jason has it bad. Seeing Kyra for the first time stirred up something in him. At first, he thought it was hatred, but when he discovers his feelings are close to the opposite, he is already far into her.

Soon, the shots they take at each

other starts building a fire of sexual tension and Jason, knowing getting into a relationship with Kyra would affect his peace of mind and probably the business, he can't seem to keep his hands off her.

Their relationship soon becomes one built on lust and hatred for one another. Will Kyra fall in love with her racist boss and will Jason be able to look past her skin color?

Find out what happens to Kyra and Jason in this hot new BWWM Romance!

READ NEXT

KISSER

Dr. Dexter Brody was a very successful dentist and was something of a ladies man. Owning one of the most thriving dental clinics in NYC, he wasn't short of female attention. But all the women he met lately were dull, boring and ordinary, until he meets Tia Michaels.

Tia the beautiful, black patient of his was unlike anyone he has ever met before, and she's even more captivating when his regular charms don't work so well on her.

Read what happens to Dexter and Tia in this HOT new Black Woman White Man Romance!

Savannah Kole is an emerging author of Romance and Contemporary Modern Fiction. Savannah has a wide range of writing interests and is currently living the incognito digital lifestyle.

Savannah is publishing books for your personal enjoyment only, especially if you like: Black Women White Male Romance, Alpha Male Curvy Women Romance, and short story series.

OTHER BOOKS PUBLISHED
BY ARDENT ARTIST BOOKS
PEN AUTHORS

Emma DaSilva
The Demon Princess
Spellcasters - The Wizards of Roseburn
Curse of The Sapphire - Limited Comic
Book Series

Harper Grast
A Werewolf's Heart

Raelynn Faith
Sweet Treats

ZT Oser
Kenyan Sunset

114

ARDENT ARTIST
BOOKS
Publishing